TINY *the* TERRIER

TINY *the* TERRIER

LINDA KEMPTON

Illustrated by **Chris Chapman**

mammoth

For Thomas Kempton with happy memories of
Pancake Day in Darley Park
L.K.

To Sam
C.C.

First published in Great Britain in 1999 by Mammoth
an imprint of Egmont Children's Books Limited
239 Kensington High Street, London W8 6SA

Text copyright © 1999 Linda Kempton
Illustrations copyright © 1999 Chris Chapman

The rights of Linda Kempton and Chris Chapman to be
identified as the author and illustrator of this work have
been asserted by them in accordance with the
Copyright, Designs and Patents Act 1988

ISBN 0 7497 3503 1

10 9 8 7 6 5 4 3 2

A CIP catalogue record for this book is
available from the British Library

Printed in Great Britain by Cox & Wyman Ltd,
Reading, Berkshire

Contents

1 *No dogs allowed!*

TOM WAS THINKING about The Plan when he first noticed the dog. He felt a sudden sharp pang for his own dog, Tinker, who had died a few months ago.

What on earth was the animal doing?

He shook a puzzled head as the little black and white terrier ran through the open door of the museum. He knew that no dogs were allowed in there except guide dogs. 'And it's certainly not a guide dog,' he muttered to himself. 'Not unless they use fox terriers nowadays.'

1

But Tom couldn't keep himself from smiling at the dog's confidence: it looked as though it owned the place. Its head and tail were held high, its tongue lolled from its mouth as if it were grinning at everyone, and its four smart white paws trotted briskly.

The park was busy today and for a moment or two, Tom lost sight of the dog. Crowds of holiday-makers strolled in the hot August sunshine and, although Tom was surrounded by people, he felt alone. If it hadn't been for The Plan he would have felt completely at a loss.

His friends had all gone

away on holiday while he was left behind in the park. For Markeaton Park was Tom's home: his father was head gardener here and Tom had lived all his life in a cottage in the grounds.

Suddenly Tom spotted the dog again. It sat on its haunches and grinned at him through the floor-to-ceiling window of the museum.

'You cheeky little thing!' Tom grinned back at the dog as he headed for the museum's open door. The building had been converted from the old stables and coach house and it was as familiar to Tom as his own front room.

Inside the building Tom walked towards the window. But when he got there the dog had vanished. There was absolutely no sign of it. He walked the length of the building but still he couldn't see it.

'Afternoon, Thomas. Come to see the sights?' Mrs Smiley looked after the museum and was an old friend of Tom's.

'No, I came to find out who the dog belongs to.'

'What dog? There's no dogs allowed in here. You know that.'

'But I saw one,' said Tom. 'Sitting in the window. A little black and white dog.'

Mrs Smiley shook her head. 'Must have strayed away from its owner: trotted in then trotted out again. I'd have shown it the door if I'd seen it.'

Tom nodded. 'I just thought I'd check.'

He pushed his hands into his pockets and wandered back the way he'd come. There was a lot of chatter; a little girl's persistent voice rose above it.

'Why is that thing all broken, Mummy?'

The little girl was pointing to the old coach, wrecked in an accident over a hundred years ago and never repaired. Now it was kept as a sort of memento.

He tried to look at the coach as if he'd never seen it before, the way his art teacher at school told them to look at things. What did the little girl see as she looked at it for the first time?

It must have been a grand coach once. Its navy blue paint was still shiny and the red-gold coat of arms, with two lions and a shield, was as bright as the day it was painted. But the door was off its hinges and two of the enormous wheels were stacked against the body of the coach. Tom knew that if he stepped over the rope cordon and went round the back, he would see the great scratches where the coach had been dragged along the road.

'It says here that there was an accident in the park and the lady of the house was killed,' said the little girl's mother.

'What else does it say? What else does

it say?' The little girl
pulled at her mother's
arm and jumped up
and down impatiently.

'Why don't you read it for yourself?'
her mother asked. She stepped back so
that her daughter could get closer. Tom
listened half-heartedly.

'There was a great storm,' the little girl
said, bending to read the card. 'And a
giant oak crashed into the path of the
carriage causing a terrible accident. The
coachman was killed too.' She seemed
delighted by the fact.

Tom felt a hand on his shoulder and
turned to see Mrs Smiley. But she was
looking at the visitors, not at Tom.

'Do you see this young man here?' Mrs Smiley pointed at Tom, and the girl looked up at him. Tom felt himself blush. He could tell Mrs Smiley was going to give one of her embarrassing speeches. 'Well, his great-great-grandfather, Jeremiah Goodall, was first on the scene after the coach crashed. Him and his fox terrier. Wasn't he, Tom?'

Tom nodded mutely.

Mrs Smiley led the mother and daughter to some photographs on the

wall and pointed to an old brown one of Jeremiah Goodall surrounded by horses and fox terriers. 'So you could say all this is part of Tom's own history.' Mrs Smiley patted Tom on the shoulder as if he deserved all the credit.

'Jeremiah Goodall of course was the one who started breeding the fox terriers. You've heard of the Markeaton fox terriers, haven't you?' Mrs Smiley put her head on one side expectantly.

The woman shook her head and smiled politely. Tom wished he could think of an excuse to get away. The little girl was staring at him.

'Won lots of dog shows over the years. And the Goodalls have carried on breeding fox terriers ever since. Tom's mother was the last to breed them, more's the pity.'

Tom felt himself go red again. Shut up, Mrs Smiley. Shut up! He didn't want to think about his mother.

'Oh yes. Where there's a Goodall there's a fox terrier. Isn't there, Tom?'

Not any more there wasn't. Oh no. Tom gave a sickly sort of smile and willed Mrs Smiley to disappear.

'Come on, Mummy, I want an ice-cream.' Tom could almost have kissed the little girl. Saved by an ice-cream! Mrs Smiley hurried back to her place behind the counter so that she could serve them.

Tom looked up at Jeremiah Goodall

and his dogs. Every night Tom prayed for another dog, another fox terrier. But one never came. Only other people's dogs in the park. Before she left, Mum had been talking about getting another dog, but when she knew she was going to have a baby she stopped. At the time he'd rather have had a dog than a baby. Now he hadn't got either. Nor had he got . . . Tom bit his lip, then took a deep breath: at least there was The Plan. Not long to wait now.

Better get home. The museum would be closing soon and Dad would be getting tea ready. He didn't like Tom to be late.

Retracing his steps, Tom sauntered towards the old coach. And there was the dog, leaning against one of the great wooden wheels. Her pink underbelly was exposed and Tom could see that she was a bitch: two rows of well-developed teats showed that she'd fed a few puppies in her time. Her watery brown eyes gazed up at Tom, and she brushed her tail silently against the floor.

Tom crouched down and put out his hand. 'Hey, girl, can't you read? It says no dogs allowed.'

The dog wagged her tail again, her eyes

still fixed on Tom's face.

She was a funny little dog, Tom thought. She had a completely white body and a completely black head, as though someone had painted her and run out of white when they reached the head. Tom liked the idea. 'Who's been painting you, eh, girl?'

Whoever it was hadn't bothered to give her a collar.

'No collar, and no name. You're an anonymous dog, No-Name, Nonny-Name . . . Nonnymous. That's it! Nonymous Dog!' Tom grinned.

Nonymous Dog wagged her tail even faster but otherwise didn't move. Tom stepped forward to stroke her and instantly she stepped back out of the way of his hand. But her eyes never left his face.

'All right, all right, Nonny. I'm not going to hurt you.'

Suddenly the dog turned her back on Tom and scrabbled at the door of the coach. Standing on her hind legs, the little dog whined and whined.

'You can't get in there, you silly old thing,' said Tom. Something about the dog's eagerness made Tom want to pick her up and hug her. But as soon as he tried to get near, the dog jumped down and backed off.

'What's the matter, Nonymous Dog? Why won't you let me stroke you?'

The dog whined again. She looked at Tom wistfully, her ears flat against her face, as if she was unhappy. Tom felt a strange tugging sensation in his stomach. The little dog *was* unhappy. Somehow he just knew she was.

2   *A howl in the night*

'DINNER'S READY!' DAD opened the sitting-room door and smiled across at Tom. 'Dreaming again? I've been calling you for ages.'

'Sorry.'

'Well tonight's delight is casseroled vegetables with pine kernels and grated cheese.' He leaned against the kitchen doorway with his hands in a pair of oven gloves, his dark hair almost brushing the top of the door frame.

Casseroled vegetables? Tom thought to himself. What's wrong with stew, like

Mum used to make? But he didn't say anything. Dad tried so hard to make him happy, to make him forget. But how could he? Especially when he knew that Dad was unhappy himself. Sometimes he heard him tossing and turning in bed, unable to sleep. Once or twice Tom had crept downstairs in the middle of the night, and found Dad sitting on the sofa with his hands knotted together, staring into space.

Tom strolled into the kitchen, wondering just how revolting dinner was going to be.

'Ta-ra, ta-ra!' Dad pulled the lid off the casserole dish. 'Would Sir like to try a little of the chef's latest culinary triumph?'

Tom smiled obediently. The weather

was far too hot for a casserole. Steam rose in great swathes from the dish. 'What did you say was in it? Pine needles?'

Dad threw his head back and laughed. 'They'd be a bit tough on the old throat, Thomas. Pine *kernels*, was what I said.'

Why do adults always laugh at what you say? Tom wondered. Why are needles funnier than kernels? They wouldn't laugh at another adult if they made a mistake: that would be bad manners. Oh yes.

'What's the matter with you, Grump-Face?' Dad pushed gently at Tom's foot under the table.

'I want a dog,' Tom replied, to his own amazement. Why had

he said that? He felt himself go red. Still, he'd said it now; may as well make the most of it. 'Can I have a dog, please, Dad?'

'No. Next question?'

Tom swung his legs backwards and forwards and stared at his pine kernels.

'Sorry, Tom. I'm out all day and you're at school most of the time. Who'd look after it?'

'Other people manage.'

'Yes, they do. But I wouldn't be happy leaving a dog all day. I'd like another one too, you know.'

'It could stay with you while you worked in the park.'

'Possibly. But I don't have time to train

a dog right now. We couldn't have it digging up the flowerbeds.'

'It would be all right if Mum came back.'

'Yes, it would. But we don't know when that's going to be,' said Dad. 'And we can't make any plans until we do know.'

But I have made a plan, thought Tom.

'Why don't we ever go and see her? We know where she's living. You write to her. I write to her.' Tom knew this last part wasn't true. He'd written to her once, after she'd first gone, but then every time he picked up pen and paper he found he just didn't know what to say; wasn't even sure he wanted to speak to her any more. Even though she was his mum and he

loved her.

He shoved a courgette angrily to the other side of his plate. Tomato juice splashed on to the bare wood of the table and Tom saw his father frown. For some reason that pleased him.

'We don't go to see her because I made a promise to stay away until she is ready to come back.'

'When will that be?' Tom pushed his chair away from the table. Why was he having this conversation now, when he had The Plan and tomorrow everything would be all right anyway?

'I don't know, Tom. I don't suppose Mum knows either.'

Then Tom felt a flash of anger so sharp,

so deep, that he couldn't hold it in. He found himself shouting and it felt clean and good. 'I hate pine needles! And I hate this stupid dinner!'

Tom lifted his plate high above his head and let the mess of courgettes, tomatoes, cheese and pine kernels slide to the floor. He banged the plate down hard and watched the remaining drops of tomato juice splash into the air. It felt like the best, the most exhilarating thing he'd done in a long time.

Then he looked at Dad's face. To his horror, he saw that his father was trying to blink back tears.

His face was red and he was biting his lip. Tom's exhilaration died.

'I'm sorry, Dad.'

Dad put out his hand and pulled Tom gently towards him. 'I'm sorry too, Tom.' He gave a deep sigh. 'You've had a rotten time just lately and I've been too busy to help much.'

'It's not your fault. You have to go to work.'

His father nodded, his colour returning to normal. 'Yes, I do. But I wish I could make things better for you.'

'You make nice meals for me. Pine needles and things.' Tom saw his father's mouth begin to twitch, and then to smile.

Soon he was giggling like a little boy.

Tom rested his cheek on top of Dad's head and felt himself smile; felt the anger drain away like water from a sink. 'I love you, Dad,' he said.

'Love you too, Tom.' Dad reached up and stroked Tom's hair.

Tom stood, his head still resting on Dad's, feeling sleepy. He ought to go to bed: he must be ready for tomorrow. He felt a surge of excitement when he thought about The Plan; there were still things to be done, things to get ready. 'I'm going to bed now,' he said.

'Goodnight, Tom. Sleep well.'

' 'Night.'

'And, Tom?'

'What?'

'They're pine kernels not pine needles.'

Very funny! Tom grinned as he ran upstairs. His dad was all right.

At the top of the stairs he stopped; he felt a pang of sadness for Dad, at what he was about to do. But he had to do it. He had to!

Tom pushed the catch that locked his bedroom door. Then he went over to the wardrobe and kneeled down to open the drawer at the bottom. His rucksack lay inside and he pulled it out so that he could check the contents once more:

wallet with money, spare pants and socks, swimming trunks and towel (he'd need those at the seaside), birthday card and timetable.

Tom sat on the bed and opened the timetable. He looked at the blue-circled numbers yet again: the bus for Brinster would leave at ten-thirty. By twelve-thirty he'd be there. He put the timetable to one side and picked up the birthday card.

It had 'To A Wonderful Mum' written on the front, with a border of red roses that looked so perfect he could almost smell them. He lifted the card to his face and sniffed. He remembered his mum's smell: sweet like Dolly Mixtures. Mum used to laugh and tell him he wasn't allowed to eat

her even if she did smell like his favourite sweets. He hadn't written anything in the card yet: he didn't know what to say.

He leaned back against the headboard and sighed. Just one more night and he would be there. He felt his eyes begin to droop.

He dreamed that the little dog had followed him home, walking alongside him and licking his hand.

Then suddenly he was awake. He sat bolt upright. He felt as though something was watching him. He looked round the room. Nothing of course. He'd locked the door and he was alone. But the feeling wouldn't go away. He stood up and went

27

to the window.

Daylight was beginning to fade, but he could still make out the little dog sitting on the lawn and looking straight up at his bedroom window. She must have followed him home. Nonymous Dog was waiting for him.

He watched her throw back her head and send out a cry that made the hair prickle on his head. The sound seemed to be coming from a long, long way, as though the dog was on the other side of the park. It was a faint echo of a howl. And it was meant for him.

Slowly Tom turned and headed for the

bedroom door. He pushed the catch and then tiptoed silently down the stairs and out of the back door.

As soon as the dog saw him she wagged her tail. Then she turned and ran. When she reached the garden hedge she stopped and looked at Tom, as if checking that he was following. A moment later she was gone.

Tom followed the dog into the park. She was running way ahead of him towards the cafeteria and museum. Tom's breath caught in his chest as he tried to keep up.

Nonymous did not stop until she reached

the old stables. She leaned against the museum door as if she wanted to push it open. And she kept her eyes on Tom who was slowing down as he reached her. She whined and scratched at the door.

'You can't go in there, Nonny. It's locked.' He bent down to pat her, but the little dog backed away.

'You're a funny old thing, aren't you?' said Tom. 'You want me to come with you but you won't let me near.'

The dog pricked up her ears and trotted along by the glass side of the museum. She stopped opposite the coach and pressed her nose up to the glass. She whimpered softly to herself.

What was she looking for? Why was she so sad?

3 *Nonny comes too*

NEXT MORNING TOM didn't have time to think about the dog. He had to move quickly if he was to catch the bus and succeed with The Plan.

When he got to the bus station the bus was already there. The palms of his hands were sweating when he handed the money to the driver and asked for his fare. He was sure his voice shook too. He hoped the driver hadn't noticed; he didn't want to arouse suspicion.

But the bus driver cocked his head to

one side and gestured towards Tom's feet. 'And what about the dog? She needs a  ticket. Just because she's only a little'n don't mean she can get away with it.'

Tom felt his stomach leap as he looked down into the little dog's face. She was panting happily and her eyes were gleaming.

'She's not mine,' he protested. But it felt like a betrayal.

'She'd better get off then,' the driver said. 'Go on, shoo her off for me.' The driver put the bus into gear and Tom heard the shush of the automatic doors.

He looked round in panic. The driver

hadn't given him time! But there was no sign of Nonymous Dog; she must have nipped off quickly.

Tom walked towards the back of the bus and saw that she hadn't. She sat on the back seat grinning as if she owned the place. Tom grinned back. Nonymous Dog was a character, as Mrs Smiley would have said!

The bus wound through country lanes and the sun shone hotly through the window so that Tom felt sleepy and unreal. Yet beneath that feeling, excitement ticked like a wound-up clock. Soon he would

see Mum again. Why hadn't he done this before? He hugged himself tightly. He should have done this weeks ago!

Tom was the only passenger on the bus. The driver whistled softly to himself and Tom half-listened, finding the whistling soothing, almost hypnotic. He thought a lot about Mum and what she would say when she saw him. He imagined the smile of surprise on her face, her arms outstretched to hold him. Aunty Doris would be there too. It would be nice to see Aunty Doris again. But it was Mum he was going to see; it was Mum he wanted. He nodded off to sleep, thinking about her.

But he woke suddenly, the hairs prickling on the back of his neck. He had that sensation again, of being watched, just like he'd had in his bedroom last night.

Tom turned quickly. The dog was watching him, not panting now, but with that wistful expression on her face that seemed to find an echo in Tom; it was as if he was feeling the dog's sadness for her.

He was shuffling round in his seat when his eye caught the driver's mirror. The driver was glaring at him.

'It's not the first time I've come across that trick,' he called. 'You just come and pay for that dog and be thankful I'm not going to report you for evading the fare.'

Tom blushed. He fumbled in the pocket of his jeans for some extra cash. He didn't want to disown the dog again; she seemed to have adopted him.

'How much is it?' Tom tottered unsteadily towards the front of the bus.

'Half-fare, same as yourself. And could you get her off the seat, please? Some people don't like white dog hair on their best clothes.'

Tom nodded and blushed again. Wretched dog! She wasn't even his!

'Get down, girl.' Tom tried to coax the dog from the seat but she gazed at him unblinkingly. 'Come on! You'll get me into trouble.' Tom put his hand out for the dog's collar, then remembered she wasn't wearing one. What was he going to do about her? Somebody would be missing her: perhaps a child or an old person living alone.

The little dog jumped down as his hand came near. 'You don't like being touched, do you, Nonymous?' Tom said. And as he said it, he noticed there wasn't a trace of a white hair on the seat.

Brinster was a small place: blink and you'd miss it. Everything was crowded together on one side of the street. On the other side were the beach and the sea. Tom lifted his nose and sniffed. You could smell it, he thought; you'd know from the salty tang in the air that you were by the seaside. He almost allowed himself to enjoy it. Almost.

He walked past
shops with beach
balls, buckets and
spades and plastic
windmills hanging
outside. Past cafés, amusement arcades,
and a small fairground with half a dozen
rides. Then he reached the chip shop.

There was no time to sit at the tables
inside, he was in too much of a hurry.
Tom pushed a can of Coke into the
pocket of his jeans and ate the chips as he
went along. He offered one to Nonymous
Dog but she backed away. He'd never
known a dog refuse food before.

Tom finished the chips and pushed the
wrappings into a bin. He swigged at his

Coke and noticed an old man shuffling towards him. He didn't look like a holiday-maker, so perhaps he lived here.

'Excuse me,' Tom said, 'do you know a place called Rose Cottage? On the cliff-top path?'

'Oh aye,' the old man said. 'It's about twenty minutes' walk from here. Just follow the road round thataway,' the old man pointed back the way Tom had come, 'past a row of bungalows, and you come to a cottage all by itself, right on the cliff top. You can't miss it.'

'Thank you. Bye.'

The old man raised his hand in farewell. 'Nice dog you got there. I've always been fond of fox terriers. Mind how you go.'

Tom walked quickly with Nonymous Dog trotting at his heels as if she belonged there.

He was half-aware of children on the beach; he could hear their laughter and hear the sounds of bats and balls. He could see bright seaside colours out of the corner of his eye. But he couldn't concentrate on anything now except finding Mum. A tight knot of tension twisted in his stomach and he began to feel sick. He wished he hadn't eaten the chips.

A woman on the beach made his heart gallop. It was Mum! But then she turned and he saw that it wasn't. Not a bit like Mum really.

He stopped walking and began to run. He ran past the bungalows and then he couldn't see anything else, just a winding path that didn't seem to lead anywhere.

Suddenly a big black dog appeared along the path and ran towards Nonymous. It snarled and growled. The hackles along its thick, black coat rose in an angry, stiff ridge and it began to bark. Tom was afraid for the little dog and put out his hand to protect her. But Nonymous seemed unconcerned. She trotted along without a sideways glance, almost as if the

big dog didn't exist. Eventually it lost interest and ran back the way it had come.

Tom shook his head. 'You're weird,' he told her, almost completely out of breath by now. He slowed to a walking pace.

The two walked on together, side by side. But the nearer Tom got, the more excited and nervous he became. Walking couldn't contain his feelings which seemed to be spilling out of him. He began to run again and ran until sweat poured beneath his T-shirt, until he couldn't run any further. Then he reached the top of the cliff and saw Aunty Doris's stone cottage standing all by itself. It had roses round the door like something from a picture book.

He saw a wooden sign on the gate, saying Rose Cottage. And when he looked down the narrow drive at the side of the cottage, he saw Mum's red sports car parked there. She was in! What would she say when she saw him?

Tom pushed at the gate and ran down the path. He peered into one of the downstairs windows but there was no sign of anybody. A framed photograph of himself stood on a dresser. It was one he'd had taken at school last year. Mum had really liked it. 'You look the spitting image of me,' she'd said proudly.

Where was she?

'Tom!'

He turned round to see Aunty Doris standing at the side of the path, a pair of secateurs in her hand.

'What on earth are you doing here, child?'

'I've come to see Mum, of course.' He heard anger in his voice. What did she think he'd come for? To see her?

'Of course you have, my love. Of course you have. I'm sorry. And you've got a dog. I never knew you had another dog.'

Aunty Doris came and gave him a big hug. Then she stood him at arm's length with her hands on his shoulders. He could feel the cold metal of the secateurs through his T-shirt.

'You get more like your mother every day; especially your eyes. You've got your mother's eyes all right.'

No he hadn't. If he had his mum's eyes he'd be able to see what she could see. He'd be able to see things through her eyes instead of his own. He'd be able to understand.

'And how long have you had this little thing?' Aunty Doris gestured towards Nonymous who was sniffing round the front door.

'She's not mine, she's just following me.'

'Oh.' Aunty Doris frowned. 'You'll need to sort that out then.'

Tom nodded.

'Where's Mum?'

'I'm afraid she's not here, Tom. She went off to walk the coastal path three days ago. Said she'd be away for a week.'

'But it's her birthday! I've got a card for her!' Tom didn't know what to say. His stomach churned and he began to feel sick again. His mum wasn't there and now the sunny day seemed cloudy and cold, as if an icy hand had covered the sky.

'Well, I'm about ready for a cup of tea,' said Aunty Doris. 'And I've some walnut cake if you've a mind.'

Tom nodded. He didn't really know what else to do. He hadn't thought that Mum would be away.

Nonymous Dog was sniffing around Mum's car and whining. She jumped up at the door.

'Now, now, you'll scratch that nice red paintwork. Get her off, can you, Tom? She'll ruin that car.'

'Down, girl. Down!'

The dog jumped down and looked at him dejectedly. Again there was that feeling of sadness between them. Tom shook his head. Why was she hanging around Mum's car? Why was she hanging around him?

'Can she come in, Aunty Doris?'

'Yes, if she wipes her feet.' Aunty Doris smiled.

But Nonymous wouldn't come in. She refused to budge from the side of Mum's car. She lay with her nose on her paws looking at Tom.

'You'll just have to stay there then,' he told her.

Aunty Doris came out with a bowl of water for Nonymous but the dog wouldn't even sniff at it.

In the house Tom sat with a huge slice of walnut cake and a glass of home-made lemonade.

'I've never had home-made lemonade before,' Tom said. 'It's really nice.'

Aunty Doris beamed. 'Can't beat it,' she said. 'Not like that muck they sell you at the supermarket. Call that lemonade!'

Tom looked round the room. He felt empty. He wanted Mum. He'd planned this for so long: how it would be, what they would say to each other. Now that he was in the place where she was staying, so near to her, he missed her more than ever. He'd ticked off thirty-five days on his calendar since she'd gone. He thought this would be the last. To his horror he felt his eyes sting and his throat smart. He was going to cry.

'I've got to go.' Tom jumped up suddenly and made a great show of checking his rucksack, his back to Aunty Doris so that she couldn't see his face.

'But you've only just arrived, love. Let me phone your dad and tell him you'll stay the night.'

'No, it's all right,' said Tom. 'It won't take me long to get home.'

Aunty Doris put her arm round him.

'Will she come home, d'you think?'

Aunty Doris squeezed his shoulder. 'Of course she will, Tom. These things take time.'

How much time? Tom wondered.

Mum had been on a visit to Aunty Doris when the baby had arrived early. She would have been a sister for him if she had lived, but she had died. Tom found that idea hard to understand. Afterwards Mum had been so upset that she had stayed with Aunty Doris. Stayed and stayed and stayed. He wished she hadn't. The baby might be dead but he was still here! He still needed Mum!

'I wish I knew how to help you, my love.' Aunty Doris leaned across and kissed him awkwardly on the cheek.

'I've got to go,' said Tom. His arms and legs, his whole body in fact, felt heavy.

'All right, love. There's a bus leaves from the station at half past. You'll just catch it if you hurry. I'll phone your dad and let him know you're on your way. He'll be worried.'

'Will you give this to Mum?' Tom pulled the birthday card from his rucksack. It was slightly crumpled now and Tom felt angry with himself for letting it get spoiled.

'She'll be thrilled to bits,' said Aunty Doris. She propped the card against the clock on the sideboard.

'Oh, hang on a minute. I haven't written in it.'

Aunty Doris handed him a pen and he stood thinking for a few moments. In the end he just wrote:

To My Best Mum,
Love Tom. xxx

Tom found himself as anxious to get home again as he had been to get to Rose Cottage. It was weird.

But Nonymous Dog didn't want to leave Mum's car. She scratched at the door, just like she had at the door of the coach. Even so, she whined after Tom as he walked down the path away from her. Tom stopped at the gate. 'Look, you've got to come, you're miles from home.'

'Go on, shoo now!' Aunty Doris clapped her hands at the dog and Nonny jumped up as the woman approached. Reluctantly, her tail tucked between her legs, she followed Tom to the gate.

'Come on, girl. You've got to come, you know.' She pricked her ears up and her tail lifted slightly. 'That's a good girl.'

When Tom reached the top of the cliff path he turned and waved to Aunty Doris. He stared at the empty cottage behind her. Mum seemed further away from him than she'd ever been.

The little dog looked up at Tom as he strode towards the bus station. She sniffed the wind and trotted obediently at his heels.

She lay beside him all the way home on

the bus, then jumped down the steps in front of him when they arrived. Dad was waiting for them, and Tom looked down as he started to explain about Nonny. But it was too late. Nonymous Dog had gone.

4 *The storm*

LATER THAT NIGHT a small shadow slipped into the garden of the cottage at Markeaton Park.

Tom was only half asleep. He'd been disturbed by growls of thunder in the distance. He opened his eyes in the darkness and saw the luminous figures on his bedside clock: 22:00. Ten o'clock.

Now another sound made him hold his breath; a small sound, the sound of scratching at his bedroom door. For a moment he couldn't move. What was it?

He threw back the duvet and jumped out of bed. But when he got to the door he was afraid to open it; afraid of what he might see. Then, before he had chance to change his mind, he pulled quickly at the bedroom door.

A small black face looked up at him. A small white body stood at his feet on the night-time landing. Then Nonymous Dog turned and trotted down the stairs. At the bottom she stopped to look up at him. He couldn't see her black face in the dark; only her white body and the glint of her eyes. But Tom knew that once again she wanted him to follow her.

This time fear held him back. How had she got in? The door was shut and locked.

Almost immediately he had his answer as his eyes registered what his brain refused to believe: Nonymous Dog faded away through the locked front door.

Tom must have stood there for ages, looking at the spot where she had disappeared. Then, in a daze, he turned and walked back to his bed. But before he could climb in, a noise drew him to the window. He pulled the curtains and saw the dog in the moonlight; almost simultaneously, he heard her begin to bark. The barking had a strange quality, as though it was coming through a tunnel from a long way off; it was frantic yet muffled.

Tom could hardly breathe. He thought about the first time he'd seen Nonny, only the day before; about the way she just appeared and disappeared. The black dog on the cliff path had been frantic at the sight of her. She didn't eat. She didn't drink. She wouldn't let him touch her. And there'd been no white hairs on the seat of the bus.

Tom rubbed his arms and shivered. He began to pull on his clothes. Nonny needed him. And Tom knew, though he didn't know how he knew, that she had chosen him specially.

The wind had risen. It moaned through the branches of the trees and rattled doors and windows. Rain slashed through the air and clouds scudded across the moon, whipped by the fierce, loud wind. The storm had broken. Jagged lightning rent the sky and the early growls of thunder had become a giant's angry booms.

Nonymous Dog moaned and howled so that her echoing voice married the wind and sang its tune.

Tom scrabbled under the bed for his trainers.

Dad moaned in his sleep and Tom hesitated at his bedroom door. He musn't disturb him.

When Tom tried to open the back door, the wind almost tore it from his grasp. Gasping, he stepped out into the storm. Almost immediately the rain sank through his clothes and pounded against his skin.

Tom followed the dog across the park. But the going was slow. The wind hit him sideways so that he had to struggle to stand. The rain stung his eyes so that he had to screw them up against it. He could hardly see.

The wind was screaming now. Trees cracked and creaked under its onslaught and broken branches sailed through the air. Tom looked at the big black trees surrounding him and knew that he was in danger. Wind like this could uproot a giant oak. Don't go near the trees in a storm, Tom. No, Dad.

'But this time I have to,' Tom whispered. 'Because something's wrong and Nonny's trying to tell me what it is.' He could still just about see the white body through the driving rain.

Water ran from his body in rivulets and his feet squelched inside his trainers. His nose ran, but it was only another wet part of him. His ears and face were stinging with cold and his head ached from the wind's battering.

It was then Tom realised that the howling of the wind was not the only

sound. A sound that he couldn't identify was bearing down on him, getting nearer, becoming louder. He strained hard to understand; then he realised that what he could hear was the galloping sound of horses' hooves and the creaking of . . .? Of what?

Tom ran towards the road, towards the sound, aware suddenly of his heart's

rhythm; aware that he was afraid. He ran from one tree to the next, trying to keep himself in shadow, not wanting to be seen. But by what he didn't know.

There was a giant cedar with low branches not more than a couple of metres from the road: the perfect hiding place. He reached it just as the noise seemed to be almost on top of him.

Then another noise: the sound of horses whinnying and crying, the sound of a dog barking and barking and barking.

Suddenly a great black shape hurtled towards him through the darkness. A flash of lightning made night seem like day, and Tom saw an old-fashioned coach and horses lurching terrifyingly from side to side. The coachman wore a black cloak and hat and Tom saw that he was shouting to the horses, his mouth forming words that the wind snatched away.

And then Tom saw the coat of arms on the side of the coach: a red-gold crest with two lions and a shield. 'It's the coach!' he shouted. 'It's the coach!'

Nonymous Dog ran beside the coach,

barking as if she would never stop.

'Nonny! Nonny!' Tom called. 'Nonny come back!'

But the little dog didn't seem to hear.

There came a terrible crashing sound and Tom saw a great tree fall right in the path of the coach. He could only watch in horror as the horses shied and the coach lurched sideways. Banging, tearing, wood splintering, horses stumbling and crying, someone screaming. A woman. Tom covered his ears. The coach wheels span. Nonny jumped on to the coach and pawed at the door with frantic yelps.

From the opposite direction came a different noise; something lower and throatier. As the noise grew louder, the coach and its horses faded as if they had never been. It was then that Tom knew he was watching something which had happened over a hundred years ago, something which was being re-enacted tonight. And as he remembered, something else came to mind about that old, old story: there had been a dog. One of Jeremiah Goodall's fox terriers had tried to save the lady of the house; the lady she had loved.

He could hear Mum's voice in his memory. 'I was born on the anniversary of that coach crash, Tom.' It wasn't midnight yet. It was still Mum's birthday.

Tom looked up to see a low red sports car winding its way down the road towards him. At the same time a jagged flash of yellow lightning illuminated the park. A terrifying crack ripped across the sky and a giant oak lurched across the road. It was going to hit Mum's car.

Almost instantly Tom saw Nonymous Dog racing towards it, along the grass at the side of the road, the gap between animal and car closing rapidly. Suddenly Nonny left the grass and turned deliberately, almost at right angles, straight into the path of the oncoming car. It came straight at her, a metre

away, no more. There was a scream of brakes and the car swerved off the road. Seconds later it came to a stop.

Tom put his head down and ran, pumping his arms and legs like pistons against the wind. Within seconds he had reached Mum's car. But as he reached for the door he felt a wave of sickness wash over him; a ringing noise played in his ears and he felt himself falling through rain. The last thing he heard was his mother's voice calling his name.

5 Next morning

WHEN TOM WOKE up next morning, watery sunlight streamed through his window. He could hear a strange snuffling noise which seemed to be coming from the foot of his bed.

He turned his head towards it and saw his mother sitting in the old wicker chair with the battered red cushion.

'Mum?'

The snuffling continued as he watched his mother rise from the chair and move towards him. She pushed back the hair from his forehead and planted a kiss there.

'Are you back?' he asked.

She smiled. 'Looks like it.'

Tom screwed up his eyes as an image flashed into his mind, of Mum's car swerving across the road.

'What happened to the car? And you? Are you all right? Are you staying? Are you going away again?' Panic rose in his chest as he heard the questions tumbling from his mouth.

'Tom, I am never, ever going away again. I promise. When I left Aunty Doris's house to spend those few days walking, I was almost certain that it was time to come home. I only did half the walk. Once I'd made up my mind, I wanted to get back to you as soon as I could.'

She held his hand and he turned his head away so she wouldn't see the tears springing to his eyes. It was quiet in the room, apart from the curious snuffling noise.

'Are you all right, then?' Tom managed to ask.

'I'm perfectly all right. The car needs a new door but nothing more than that.'

Scratched and dented, just like the coach. Where was Nonymous Dog?

'Mum, there's this dog. I've got to tell you.'

So he did. He told her everything. Everything.

Mum nodded. 'I saw the dog. That's

what made me swerve. She probably saved my life. Dad and I looked all round for her afterwards.' She looked at Tom with a strange look in her eyes; he felt as though there was something more she wanted to say. 'I didn't really expect to find her.' She reached out and took Tom's hand.

'What's that noise?' The snuffling was growing louder.

Mum grinned. 'I bought myself a birthday present. I thought maybe you and Dad would like to share it too.'

Mum walked to the foot of the bed and bent down, so that Tom couldn't see her. When she stood up she was holding something in her arms. Something with a wet little nose and a furry black face.

Tom swallowed. He knew he ought to say something, but his body seemed so full he felt it might burst if he spoke. He knew there was a grin wandering somewhere round his face but he didn't have any control over it.

'Isn't she lovely?' Mum put the little black and white puppy on Tom's knee. He picked her up and buried his face in her fur. She smelled like biscuits.

'She looks just like Nonny,' Tom said. And she did. Her head was completely black and her body completely white. Just as if someone had painted her and run out of white at the head.

6 *Tiny the terrier*

THE STORM HAD left branches strewn across the park. Tom and his mother strode across the grass towards the road. Tom had the puppy in his arms and she was lifting her nose to sniff the wind.

'You wouldn't think a tiny puppy could get so heavy,' said Tom.

Mum took the puppy from him and snuggled her under her chin. 'Yes, they start off feeling light but seem to weigh heavier with every step you take. But we can't put her down till she's had her injections. We don't want her to catch anything.'

As they drew near the road, Tom started to feel nervous, as if he might have to relive the coach and the crash all over again. But the morning had brought sunshine and bright scudding clouds. There were lots of people about.

'They moved the car first thing,' Mum told him.

Tom nodded. He was glad.

'This poor little puppy got thrown about a bit,' said Mum. 'But she doesn't seem any the worse for it, does she?'

Tom looked at the bright-eyed little creature and smiled.

'Mind you,' Mum said, 'she made a

great big puddle and poo on the back seat, so she must have been frightened.'

'Poor little thing,' said Tom. He smiled again. 'I hope you're not going to make a habit of puddling and pooing all over the place, Puppy,' he said.

The puppy sighed and rested her head on Mum's arm.

The fallen tree took Tom by surprise. It lay across the road, its giant roots like veins across the clotted earth at its base.

It was enormous. It would have crushed the car instantly.

'All's well that ends well, Tom,' said Mum gently when she noticed the expression on his face.

When they reached the place where Mum's car had come to a stop, it was easy to see where it had been. Deep tyre marks scored the grass, and several small bushes had been flattened. Flakes of red paint were stuck to a tree-trunk.

'Good job I'd almost come to a stop by that time,' said Mum, running her hand across the paint marks.

'What was it you wanted to show me?' asked Tom.

'It's this way,' she said.

They came to a clearing and Tom saw a small mound covered with ivy. Mum kneeled down in front of it and began pulling at the ivy, wrenching handfuls away and tossing them on to the grass. As she worked, she began to uncover what looked to Tom like a small headstone. He kneeled down beside her to take a closer look.

'I just wanted you to know, Tom, that Nonymous Dog did have a name.' She sat back on her heels so that Tom could read the inscription.

TO

TINY

A FOX TERRIER

DIED AUGUST 12 1891

AGED 15 YEARS

A TRUE FRIEND

TO ALL THOSE

SHE COULD TRUST

'She trusted me,' Tom said. 'Tiny trusted me.' And Mum nodded as if she really knew. His voice wobbled and he felt a lump come to his throat. He reached over and lifted the sleeping puppy from Mum's arms. The little dog grunted contentedly. 'Can we call her Tiny? Please?'

'Of course we can, Tom. I thought you were never going to ask.' Mum smiled.

'Tiny is her grandmother; with lots of greats in front.'

At the edge of the clearing Tom turned to take a last look at the headstone. He blinked once. Then he blinked again. The ghost dog lay across her grave. Through her body, Tom could see the lettering on the stone. August 12th. Mum's birthday.

The sadness seemed to have gone from Nonymous Dog, from Tiny. He could almost have sworn she was smiling. Perhaps she was. After all, she had done what she came to do.

'Bye, Nonny,' he whispered. But even as he spoke she was becoming fainter. He looked down at Tiny's namesake, his very

own puppy, and kissed her warm head. 'Say goodbye to your great-great-great-great grandmother.'

The puppy licked his face. And when Tom lifted his head to say a last goodbye, Tiny the ghost dog had gone.

If you enjoyed this
MAMMOTH READ try:

Dead Trouble

Keith Gray
Illustrated by *Clive Scruton*

What a find! It was lying there –
just like the ones real cowboys use.

Sean and Jarrod hide the deadly
prize in their den.

Then Old Man Cooney discovers
their secret . . .

'a powerful and shocking
cautionary tale'
Gillian Cross

If you enjoyed this
MAMMOTH READ try:

The Stare

Pat Moon
Illustrated by *Greg Gormley*

Jenna can't believe it – just by staring
at someone she can make them do
whatever she likes! The results are
hilarious – not to mention chaotic!

Her best friend, Eddie, thinks it's
the most amazing gift – Jenna really
is telepathic. Then he discovers
the secret behind Jenna's
new-found talent.

But when he tries to warn her, she
just won't listen . . .

If you enjoyed this
MAMMOTH READ try:

The Lantern Fox

Garry Kilworth
Illustrated by *Chris Chapman*

April is very shy. She is much
happier fishing than talking to
people – until she meets a
lantern fox.

The fox glows from within like a
lamp, making him an easy target
for hunters. April decides to hide
him in her room until his light
fades. She has to find ingenious
ways to prevent her family
discovering her new friend.

But, gradually, as the lantern fox
begins to fade, April begins to
shine with an inner light of
her own

If you enjoyed this
MAMMOTH READ try:

The Gargoyle

Garry Kilworth
Illustrated by *Dan Williams*

An ugly stone gargoyle, which
comes to life whenever there is a
full moon, and a lonely boy,
become the best of friends.

Together they travel far away
through the darkness to find the
boy's mother.

Can they get home again before
the gargoyle turns to stone?

A spellbinding night adventure.